Priscilla

AND THE PINK PLANET

by
Nathaniel Hobbie

illustrated by
Jocelyn Hobbie

LITTLE, BROWN AND COMPANY
New York Boston

For Mom and Dad, and, of course, for Hope

Also by Jocelyn Hobbie and Nathaniel Hobbie:
Priscilla and the Splish-Splash Surprise
Priscilla Superstar!

First Paperback Edition: January 2008

Little, Brown and Company

Hachette Book Group USA
237 Park Avenue, New York, NY 10017
Visit our Web site at www.lb-kids.com

Library of Congress Cataloging-in-Publication Data

Hobbie, Nathaniel.
Priscilla and the pink planet / by Nathaniel Hobbie ; illustrated by Jocelyn Hobbie.-- 1st ed.
p. cm.
Summary: Tired of seeing the color pink, Priscilla encounters the Pink Planet's Great Queen of Pink and tries to convince her of the need for a variety of colors.
HC ISBN-10: 0-316-73579-5 / HC ISBN-13: 978-0-316-73579-7
PB ISBN-10: 0-316-11349-2 / PB ISBN-13: 978-0-316-11349-6
[1. Color—Fiction. 2. Planets—Fiction. 3. Stories in rhyme. 4. Children's writings.] I. Hobbie, Jocelyn, ill. II. Title.
PZ8.3.H655Pr 2005
[E]—dc22 2003060206

TWP

HC: 10 9 8 7 6 5 4
PB: 10 9 8 7 6 5 4 3 2 1

Printed in Singapore

Gazing up at the sky on a very clear night
you may see a star with a curious light.
Well, that star is red, to yourself you may think,
but study it close — it's a planet — it's pink!

Believe me, you must, that this planet is pink
straight through from the top to the bottom, I think.
And not only that, but every creature around
is as pink as every pebble and stone on the ground.
Every flower is pink, and so are their stems!
The eggs are all pink, as are all the hens.
Pink pillows, pink curtains, pink windows and doors.
Pink from the ceiling to the boards on the floors.

Pink apples, bananas, pink oranges, too.
    Pink bicycles, pink rubber on the sole of your shoe.
Pink rivers. Pink fish. Pink grass and pink sky.
    Pink is all you can see, no matter how hard you try.

Of all the colors, some think pink is the best.
But poor little Priscilla, she needed a rest.
She just couldn't eat one more bowl of pink porridge,
so she took all her pink things and put them in storage.

She packed up her bag with her toothbrush and comb
and a few other things to remind her of home.
Then waving goodbye, she set off to discover
somewhere on that world at least one other color.

Priscilla marched herself straight out of town,
when she came to a signpost that caused her to frown.

"Pink, pink, pink!" cried Priscilla with fright,
"Pink to the left and pink to the right.
"Pink to the left and pink to the right.
Enough pink to make you stay home, sick in bed."

But, thought Priscilla, *I could go* straight, *instead*.

Her mind was made up. Her course had been set.
She'd never stop searching, at least not just yet.
So squaring her shoulders and not looking back,
She stepped off the road to make her own track.

She meandered through meadows of Pink Fire flowers

and down into canyons with pink spiraling towers.

She climbed into treetops and crept under hedges.
She looked behind rocks and peered over ledges.

She waded through swamps that had a gurgling stink:
even that muck—you guessed it—was pink!
She circled and crisscrossed every square inch of ground,
but only one color was there to be found.

When finally she came to a great Pink Pole tree,

she threw up her hands and dropped to one knee.

"Please give me a signal. Just show me a sign.

Is there some other color in this pink world of mine?"

Suddenly, drifting, as if from thin air,
a creature appeared to answer her prayer.
A butterfly hovered at the tip of her nose.
"Oh my," gasped Priscilla, "what colors are *those*?!"

So what do you think Priscilla did next?
Sat there scratching her tummy, looking perplexed?
No sir, not Priscilla, not this little girl!
She was up on her feet in a back-flipping twirl!

Bashing through brambles, cartwheeling down ditches,
pausing just once to untangle her britches,
Priscilla did soar like a ship at full sail,
keeping close as she could to the butterfly's trail.

Then the butterfly, who'd been traveling top speed,
fluttered down for a rest on a Pink Cluster weed.
Strange, thought Priscilla, *it's the one weed around*.
And then it was clear — this was some special ground.

Fountains and flower beds and curving stone walls,
trees trimmed like pyramids and shrubs round as balls.
Then *swoosh*, out of nowhere, and quite by surprise,
a net came *down*, right in front of her eyes.

There stood a woman in a frilly long gown
with a cape and a ring and a net and a crown.
And inside the net the butterfly flapped.
Priscilla knew then and there the creature was trapped.

"Now look, little girl, just what do you think?!
Don't you know who I am?! I'm the Great Queen of Pink!
This whole planet is mine, ocean and land,
and unwelcome visitors are one thing I can't stand!"

Well, Priscilla almost ran away, right on the spot,
but the pink in her cheeks was growing quite hot.
"Miss Queen," piped Priscilla, "I've traveled so far!
May I at least take the butterfly home, in this jar?"

"Good gracious, no!" roared the Great Queen.
"This awful creature is positively obscene!
All those colors, how gaudy! How simply *passé*.
I made this planet pink and that's how it will stay!
Pink is the color that I like the best,
so take my advice and forget all the rest.
As for this creature, it's back underground,
where *all* other colors are kept, safe and sound."

Well, Priscilla just couldn't believe what she'd heard.
Hiding those colors! Good grief! How absurd!
But the Queen wasn't joking. Priscilla could tell.
How, thought the girl, *can I break the Queen's spell*?
And then an idea flashed in her mind—
the type of idea that was just the right kind.

"I agree," said Priscilla, "that pink *is* the best.
But that's hard to tell without seeing the rest.
If *all* colors were out for the wide world to see,
pink would look even pinker, don't you agree?"

The Queen seemed a bit puzzled. She scratched at her chin.
But then her face spread in an ear-to-ear grin.
"My dear little girl! Why hadn't I thought of that?!
What would be thin if something else weren't fat?
What is short without tall, big without small?
What is hot without cold, after all?
Of course we need colors. What would one color be
without all of the others for the whole world to see?"

Then the Queen waved her net to the left, to the right.
She sang out a spell about colors and light.
Then, suddenly, colors started just popping out—
every which way you looked a new color would sprout!

Priscilla gasped in amazement at the sight of green trees.
A pale purple flower made her weak in the knees.

The bright yellow sun! And the sky, it was blue!

"Oh my," cried Priscilla, "the world seems brand new!"

The Queen kissed Priscilla and patted her head.
"Dear child, you're right," was the last thing she said.
Then, poof, she was gone, as quick as she'd come,

yet Priscilla knew her adventure wasn't quite done.

"Colors!" cried Priscilla, "There's so much to see!
A world with just one—how could that be!

I love *all* colors and *all* of their hues.
I love all the reds, different yellows, and blues."

Then bursting with joy, cartwheeling with glee,
Priscilla raced home loving all she could see.